GET READY...GET SET...READ!

THE CROSSING

by
Foster & Erickson

Illustrations by
Kerri Gifford

BARRON'S

"Let's see who is best
at crossing the moat,"

said the old man
in the yellow coat.

“I hope it’s me,” said Dale.
“I’ll try with all my might.”

Then he looked around
at all the boats and said,
"This is quite a sight."

Whiptail, Dean, Gail, Colleen,
and more—they all had boats.

"Go!" said the old man
in the yellow coat.

Whiptail was first.
He set sail so fast!

But his tail whipped the sail
and then he was last.

Little Dale saw it all.
So he got out of his boat,

to carry Whiptail
across the moat.

Dean had a boat
that looked like a bean.

It would not float.
It began to lean.

Out fell Dean!
And there was Dale,

to take him across
to be with Whiptail.

Next came Gail and Raccoon
on a boat they called,
"The Yellow Moon."

"Hold tight," said Gail.
She gave some balloons
to Raccoon.

Raccoon set sail across the moat,
without Gail or the boat.

"Let go!" said Gail.
You know who found Raccoon.
It was little Dale.

Then came Moose and Loon.
They crooned a tune
that sounded like a bassoon.

"Look out!" called Dale.
But they could not hear
over the tune.

The boat hit the rock
and it would not float.

So Dale helped them both across the moat.

Then came the boat
of Coyote and Goat,
and Colleen's "Evergreen."

Dale helped them all
across the moat.
It was a sight to be seen!

Then Dale went back
for his own boat.

But he fell asleep
while crossing the moat.

"Who is best at sailing the moat?" they asked the man in the yellow coat.

"Who crossed it best is
over there.
He crossed with all his might..."

"It's Dale!" he said.
And they all knew
the old man was right.

DEAR PARENTS AND EDUCATORS:

Welcome to ***Get Ready...Get Set...Read!***

We've created these books to introduce children to the magic of reading.

Each story in the series is built around one or two word families. For example, *A Mop for Pop* uses the OP word family. Letters and letter blends are added to OP to form words such as TOP, LOP, and STOP.

This ***Bring-It-All-Together*** book serves as a reading review. When your children have finished *Whiptail of Blackshale Trail, Colleen and The Bean, Dwight and the Trilobite, The Old Man at the Moat,* and *By the Light of the Moon*, it is time to have them read this book. *The Crossing* uses some of the characters and most of the words introduced in the fourth set of five ***Get Ready . . . Get Set . . . Read!*** stories. (Each set in the series will be followed by two review books.)

Bring-It-All-Together books provide:
- much needed vocabulary repetition for developing fluency.
- longer stories for increasing reading attention spans.
- new stories with familiar characters for motivating young readers.

We have created these ***Bring-It-All-Together*** books to help develop confidence and competence in your young reader. We wish you much success in your reading adventures.

Kelli C. Foster, Ph.D.
Educational Psychologist

Gina Clegg Erickson, MA
Reading Specialist

All inquiries should be addressed to:
Barron's Educational Series, Inc.
250 Wireless Boulevard
Hauppauge, NY 11788

International Standard Book Number 0-8120-9337-2
Library of Congress Catalog Card Number: 95-51732

PRINTED IN HONG KONG
6789 9927 98765432

There are five sets of books in the

Series. Each set consists of five **FIRST BOOKS** and two **BRING-IT-ALL-TOGETHER BOOKS**.

is the first set your children should read.
The word families are selected from the short vowel sounds:
at, **ed**, **ish** and **im**, **op**, **ug**.

SET 2

provides more practice
with short vowel sounds:
an and **and**, **et**, **ip**, **og**, **ub**.

SET 3

focuses on
long vowel sounds:
ake, **eep**, **ide** and **ine**, **oke** and **ose**, **ue** and **ute**.

SET 4

introduces the idea that the word family sounds
can be spelled two different ways:
ale/ail, **een/ean**, **ight/ite**, **ote/oat**, **oon/une**.

SET 5

acquaints children with word families that
do not follow the rules for long and short vowel sounds:
all, **ound**, **y**, **ow**, **ew**.